SEABURN CITY ARE...

For Sunderland fans everywhere — it'll be ok in the end.

A TEMPLAR BOOK

First published in the UK in 2014 by Templar Publishing,
an imprint of The Templar Company Limited,
Deepdene Lodge, Deepdene Avenue, Dorking, Surrey, RH5 4AT, UK
www.templarco.co.uk

First edition

ISBN 978-1-84877-518-3 (hardback)
ISBN 978-1-78370-018-9 (paperback)

Designed by Mike Jolley
Edited by Libby Hamilton

Printed in China

SIMON BARTRAM

UP FOR THE CUP!

templar publishing

This is me, Charlie Horsewill and I LOVE FOOTBALL!

My Dad calls me a "complete and utter footie nutter", but really he's just the same. When we wear our famous red-and-yellow shirts, Mam jokes that we look just like two sticks of rock. She's right. Cut us down the middle and we would read one name all the way through... SEABURN CITY! THE ONLY TEAM FOR US!

Every home match, 49,856 fans fill our GRAND CITY STADIUM. I don't know what we'd all have done before 1879. That was when City was formed by SIR ALFRED CUMMINS, owner of the Alphabet Spaghetti Company.

Today the company is still our top team sponsor, and that's where Dad works, making the 'T's, the 'P's and the 'G's, although he'd prefer to make the 'V's because, as we always chant on match days...

V STANDS FOR VICTORY! VICTORY TO THE CITY!

Mam says winning isn't important, it's the taking part that counts. But last season even SHE couldn't contain her excitement as, for the first time EVER, Seaburn City made it all the way to...

THE CUP FINAL!

From our goalie, 'Glue Gloves' Montgomery, to our captain, Frasier Gurney, every player is a vital cog in the Seaburn City machine. But there's one player above all who we just can't do without...

JULIO POOM!

He can do things with a ball that defy scientific science. My Dad LOVES him!

He's the best thing to come out of Argentina since corned beef!

My best friend Billy Ball and his dad love him!

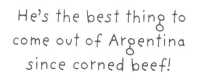

He MUST be an alien! Or at LEAST a robot!

And of course I LOVE HIM!

We all agree, he's a footballing **GENIUS!**

However, like most geniuses, Julio is a teeny-tiny bit STARK RAVING BONKERS! For a start, he has a LOT of oddball superstitions...

Before home games he HAS to ride his bike around the ticket office six times. And before away games he ALWAYS does his interviews wearing a suit of armour.

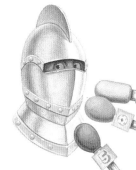

He's two chops short of a barbecue, that lad!!

BUT MOST IMPORTANTLY, before EVERY game his pre-match meal absolutely HAS to be alphabet spaghetti, so he can write in tomatoey letters: TODAY JULIO, YOU WILL SHINE LIKE A STAR.

If he doesn't spell out this special pasta message, he's convinced that some kind of footballing catastrophe will strike. And that superstition almost created the biggest disaster EVER!

FOOTIE FACTS: THE WARM-UP

Before every game, each team has its own special warm-up routine. Here we can see City players doing a typical session of Gaelic dancing.

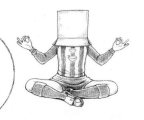

Captain Frasier Gurney prefers to meditate quietly (with a box on his head to block out the Gaelic dancing).

Finally the whole team come together to focus mind and body with an egg-and-spoon race.

SEABURN CITY

SAMSON GABBIADINI
Forward

TOMMY 'GLUE GLOVES' MONTGOMERY
Goalkeeper

SIDNEY KERR
Left-back

ALBERT CARTER
Centre midfield

DICKIE ROWELL
Right-back

BARRINGTON HURLEY
Centre midfield

RBERT QUINN-PHILLIPS
Right wing

HERBERT PORTERFIELD
Centre half

BIG CYRIL STOKOE
Manager

SEABURN CITY

FRASIER GURNEY (Captain)
Centre half

FITZGIBBON NOSWORTHY
Left wing

JULIO POOM
Centre forward

Cup Final week started well. On MONDAY, at the club shop, I bought a FANTASTIC poster of an astronaut planting a City flag on the MOON!

Dad said that certainly WOULD BE a huge leap for mankind!

On TUESDAY City Mascot Lorenzo Spaghetti visited our school. He did keepy-uppies in the yard until a sudden downpour made his spongey bowl-head too heavy to keepy-uppy and that was that!

On WEDNESDAY at Pizza Shed I gobbled down a Cup-shaped, Deep-pan, Meat-feast special. It was tip-top tasty, although Dad did complain to the waiter that the handles were COMPLETELY the wrong shape!

FRIDAY was Cup Final Eve. Before bed, I ticked off my big match checklist. Butterflies swirled around my tummy as Dad tucked me in. The waiting was almost over. JUST ONE MORE SLEEP!

On THURSDAY Dad was named 'Spaghetti Worker of the Month' and was presented with the company's 133-year-old trophy. IT WAS SURELY A SIGN! He decided to make it into a hat to wear to THE FINAL!

ESSENTIAL SUPPORTERS KIT CHECKLIST

- ☑ TICKET
- ☑ HAT
- ☑ SCARF
- ☑ STICKER SWAPS
- ☑ PAPER PLATES (MAM'S IDEA)
- ☑ TOILET ROLL (DAD'S IDEA)
- ☑ PIE MONEY

And then on SATURDAY it was here at last — CUP FINAL DAY!!! It looked like the whole singing, flag-waving city was off to the match. Everyone was SO happy... until Billy's radio broke the TERRIBLE NEWS!

"This morning the Alphabet Spaghetti Company dramatically announced that not a single letter 'O' has been produced at the factory for weeks! After receiving hundreds of customer complaints, they have discovered that the machine that makes the pasta 'O's has been SABOTAGED.

"Police believe the crime is a despicable attempt to prevent Seaburn City's JULIO POOM from spelling out his pre-match pasta goodluck message, ahead of today's Cup Final. They are looking for a Mr Roderick Nut, a fan of City's opponents, Doombarton United, who is believed to be the prime suspect.

"A nationwide search for cans containing the letter 'O' is underway. Meanwhile, at the City team's hotel, Julio Poom is said to be refusing to come out from under his bed."

The dreadful news quickly spread from van to coach to car...

Throughout the journey, fans wracked their brains for a solution...

Deep down though, everybody knew that only pasta letters would do. It was a pickle all right, but Dad said we'd just have to give Julio extra-loud support. So, as we approached the stadium, Dad popped on his trophy hat and led the POOM-POOM-POOOMINATOR singalong. Then, at long last,

WE WERE THERE!

I knew this was it — THE BIG ONE! Clicking through the turnstiles the butterflies in my stomach went crazy, and as we stepped out into the arena, only one word sprang to mind...

The pitch was smooth as a snooker table and the tops of the stands seemed closer to the moon than the Earth. All around us flags fluttered and fans sang. It was a sea of red and yellow.

As the players walked out for the Royal Presentation, we were all relieved to see Julio in the line-up. Through the deafening din smiled and gave me his 'V for victory' I smiled too and saluted right back. everything was going to be okay

But it was not to be. As the Queen shook Julio's hand, her fluffy corgis irritated his nose. With an enormous "ATTISSHOO!!" he sneezed all over Her Majesty, blowing off her tiara, which landed on a ball boy's head. 90,000 FANS GASPED!

In the end, the Queen grumpily ordered the referee to take action and so, even before kick-off, Julio was shown the yellow card. On the big screen, Julio's legs looked all wobbly. Then, as City lost the toss, he looked close to tears. When the Cup Final began at last, it was as if he'd never even SEEN a football before, never mind KICKED one.

7 MINS   13 MINS   21 MINS

It seemed Julio's pasta disaster was getting the better of him. Everything he did went wrong, and it had started to rub off on his teammates.

28 MINS

35 MINS

44 MINS

Even though the Red-and-Yellow Army were roaring like a twelfth man for the team, City manager, BIG CYRIL STOKOE, still looked worried. His top-class comb-over was unusually lifeless. I was sure only one thought could be pinging around his brain...

BLOOMIN' ALPHABET SPAGHETTI!

So far, only the United fans were having fun.
They even composed a song to tease our Julio:

YOU'RE JULIO POOM,
YOU POOR OLD SOUL,
YOU'VE GOT NO 'O'S,
YOU'RE IN A HOLE,
WELL WE'VE GOT 'O'S,
FOR YOU TO USE,
SO NOW YOU CAN SPELL
"WE'RE GONNA LOSE!"

It was an awful tune, but it spoke the truth.
If things didn't change we WERE going to lose.
But it was still 0-0 and, with half-time
fast approaching, everyone agreed
things could have been MUCH worse.
All we needed was a goal.

AND THEN, just as the referee was
about to blow the half-time whistle...

JULIO
SCORED!

With a BULLET of a header, he'd crashed the ball past the goalie and into the net. Half the stadium EXPLODED with joy. Sadly, it wasn't the City half.

IT WAS AN OWN GOAL! CITY: 0, UNITED: 1! It was HEARTBREAKING. And worse STILL, the United players celebrated in the style of my favourite heavy metal band, THE BURNING ANGRY FURIOUS CHAPS! I would never be able to listen to their music EVER AGAIN.

FOOTIE FACTS: THE GOAL CELEBRATION

Every player plans their own unique way of celebrating the moment they score a goal. These are just a few examples:

The Skyscraper.

The Burning-Angry-Furious-Chaps tribute.

The Pirouette.

The Dead Men.

At half-time Dad himself was a Burning Angry Furious Chap, mainly because he was stuck in the toilet for most of it.

HEEEEEEEEEELLLLP!!

And his mood didn't improve in the second half.
The United scoundrels were trying to CHEAT their way
to victory with dodgy diving and time-wasting tactics.
Billy was sure they'd all have been sent off had the
referee not been wearing blue-and-white underpants under his shorts.
As for City, they were getting worse and time was running out.

Dad said that he wished he was
still stuck in the toilet.

Even so, he cheered City on with all his heart. And so did everyone around us, apart from one suspicious character.

Then suddenly, in the 88th minute, the ball landed at Julio's feet. THE GOAL WAS GAPING! IT WAS ON A PLATE!

HE COULDN'T MISS!

... but miss he did.

It got worse. Having cleared the crossbar, the ball fizzed towards us and CRASHED into Dad's trophy hat, smashing it to SMITHEREENS! It was a terrible end to a truly terrible afternoon. OR SO WE THOUGHT!

You see, on gathering up the bits of trophy I made a crucial discovery.

Without its handles or base, the trophy was actually an ancient tin of food, painted silver. And what's more, there was some TOMATOEY SAUCE leaking from it. Cautiously, I lifted the lid and couldn't believe my eyes. IT WAS A 133-YEAR-OLD TIN OF ALPHABET SPAGHETTI!

AND IT HAD 'O's!!

This was our BIG chance! If Julio was desperate for a pasta boost, then it was up to US to give it to him!

But we would need the perfect hat-trick: the ancient spaghetti, our paper plates and the TV cameras to spot us at just the right moment. For once our luck was in — suddenly there we were, high up on the big screen! A huge red-and-yellow roar filled the stadium.

And down on the pitch, as City won a last-gasp corner, there was Julio, staring right up at the screen too.

He was transfixed by our pasta messages! So transfixed, he didn't notice Norbert Quinn-Phillips' corner swinging in... until it THWAAAACKED him full in the face.

The entire universe seemed to stand still. Only the ball kept on moving, straight past the goalie, over the line and into the gaping United net! It was incredible!

JULIO HAD EQUALISED!

He looked gobsmacked. On the day he expected everything to go wrong, something had gone RIGHT!

It was proof that his superstitions were codswallop! Amidst the wild celebrations I climbed onto Dad's shoulders and, amazingly, Julio spotted me. For a moment we stared at each other as if we were the only two people in the stadium.

Then Julio simply SMILED. At once he looked bigger and stronger and more determined.

OUR MESSAGES WORKED!

HE LOOKS HAPPY!

HE'S BACK!

It was true. Julio was back! He was ready to take on the world, never mind Doombarton United.
As he turned away he gave me a great big thumbs-up and I replied with a 'V for Victory' salute.

In the very last minute of the match, THE CUP FINAL HAD JUST BEGUN...

The ball was GLUED to his boots. The United players couldn't get anywhere near him. With speed and skill he shimmied through their midfield. He cut through their defence like a knife through butter. He stared into the whites of the goalie's eyes. The referee was about to blow the full-time whistle. The moment had come. For the second time that afternoon only one word sprang to mind...

As the ball CRASHED into
the back of the net, my dreams came true.
It was the last kick of the match.
It was 2-1 TO SEABURN CITY!

WE'D WON THE CUP!

I've dreamed about that
afternoon every night since.
Sometimes I can't believe that
it all actually happened,
especially the moment
when Julio beckoned me
down from the stands

to join the victory
parade. Later Billy
told me that Dad
had been fighting
back the tears.

The next morning even Mam was fighting them back when she saw me plastered all over the newspapers. On Monday I had to sign lots of autographs at school and at lunchtime we were given a celebration meal of spaghetti 'V's on toast. At work Dad was promoted — now it's his job to make the spaghetti 'V's and once in a while he sends a jumbo tin to Julio. Not that Julio relies on spaghetti any more. Now he only relies on his superskill.

I really hope that one day I will be good enough to play for City. Dad always says that practice makes perfect, so every night we have a kickabout, recreating Julio's cup-winning scorcher. And as the sun goes down, he carries me on his shoulders and we sing the 'POOM, POOM, POOMINATOR' song all the way home.

AT THE CUP FINAL, CAN YOU SPOT...

RODERICK NUT
Doombarton United fan and criminal

AGATHA CUSTARD
Seaburn City tea lady

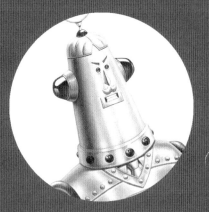

NIGEL CURRUTHERS
Galaxobot 3000, programmed to love Seaburn City

GILBERT TRUNCHEON
Voted 'Fan whose head most resembles the Cup Final trophy'

TREVOR AND PIPPA TROLLEY
Married on Cup Final day

MR BALL
Toupé-wearing father of Billy

CAROL CRAM
Great, great, great, great, granddaughter of Sir Alfred Cummins

SIMON BARTRAM
Author, illustrator and complete and utter football nutter!

BOB AND BARRY
The star of Simon Bartram's book *Man on the Moon, a Day in the Life of Bob* and his best friend Barry also went to the Cup Final. Can you spot them and the unusual (some would say alien) fans who followed them?